Apricot Ape says:
"It is nice to have friends."

ZERO WORD BOOKS FOR CHILDREN

These jungle adventures are a fun and colorful way for children to develop reading skills.

The objectives are:
1. Developing an excitment for books and reading.
2. Developing left-to-right sequencing essential for reading.
3. Developing verbal skills. Children can tell the story in their own words and on their own level.
4. Developing logical thinking.
5. Developing social skills such as teamwork, honesty, and friendship.

The titles are:
1. Apricot Ape
2. Ape Escape
3. Honest Ape
4. The Ape Team
5. Going Bananas
6. The Jungle Train

These books are great for group activity or free-time pleasure for children of all ages.

GOING APE BOOKS

The Ape Team

Story and pictures by Bob Reese

ARO PUBLISHING

DANGER
NO SWIMMING!

DANGER
NO SWIMMING!